Reindeer
of the year!

Rosie Greening · Stuart Lynch

make
believe
ideas

"Today's the day!" says **Santa**,
and the **elves** all give a **cheer**.

Every year, this contest puts the REINDEER to the test.

They each compete to win the prize
and prove they are the best!

The stadium is buzzing.

It's almost time to start.

and does a loop-the-loop.

Reindeer two is COMET,

whose fireworks crack and fizz.

He sets off zooming rockets

that go POP and BANG

Reindeer **three** is **Dancer,** who **waltzes,** hops, and **spins.**

Reindeer four is

Cupid -

the singing superstar!

Next up are the reindeer twins: performers five and six.

BLITZEN flips

and **DONDER** dives

when they do **snowboard** tricks!

Little **prancer** leaps on stage

and starts to

bounce

and **bound.**

When it comes to **high** jumps, he's the **best** reindeer around!

Up last is graceful **Vixen,**
who's the **coolest** reindeer yet.

She ice-skates round the stadium, performing pirouettes.

The audience starts **cheering**
as **confetti** fills the skies.

Every reindeer **tried** their best,
but **who** will win the **prize?**

Santa gets the shining cup and smiles around with pride.

Who is the

Reindeer of the year?

It's your turn to decide!